26.2
Trail of Truth

26.2
Trail of Truth

By Bruce Morrison

HAMPTON ROADS
PUBLISHING COMPANY, INC.

Hampton Roads Publishing Co., Inc.
891 Norfolk Square
Norfolk, Virginia 23502

Or call: 804-459-2453
    FAX 804-455-8907

Cover design by Patrick Smith
Printed in the United States of America

A Dedication

It took more than two years to complete this work. Never fully satisfied with phrases, and wanting the message to be truly meaningful to all who partake, words were polished and then polished again.

It was painful and sometimes tedious. There was agony. Some words came in the darkness, straining with closed eyes to envision and then describe that vision in words.

I imagined Phidippides struggling, dying. He completed his duty, the Greek messenger who ran the first recorded marathon.

My mother's father, William G. Altzerines, was born in a small town in the mountains of Greece, and his marathon was leaving his country and finding new hope in America. He is buried in Columbus, GA.

It is to "Papa" that this book is dedicated.

Foreword
by Harold Tinsley

Scoring that first touchdown at the beginning of a career in the National Football League or hitting that first home run in Yankee Stadium has to be a most satisfying experience, one few of us will ever realize.

Some of us, however, may have sensed what that may be like from the sports we can participate in. It could be that feeling I get poised at the top of a rapid when the current grabs the kayak and I realize there is no turning back or when I leaned back that first time at the top of a cliff, putting all my trust in the rappel rope. Words cannot do justice to convey these feelings to others. They must be experienced.

The sports event available to many, and perhaps the one which provides the most rewarding experience, is the marathon. The sense of accomplishment when you finish your first marathon is another of those impossible experiences to convey to others. I don't know of a marathoner who hasn't at least considered writing about his or her first marathon. Is this why such a high percentage come back to run another?

Bruce Morrison has gone far beyond the finish line in expressing his marathon experiences. In *26.2: Trail of Truth,* Bruce has unlocked some of the reasons why I have found the marathon experience so enthralling.

Never had I realized the parallel between the stages of a marathon and life itself. Every step along the way, the ups and downs, to survive or to give in. All the virtues of life play through the battle from start to end. Like life, you learn along the way, and in the end there is the wisdom gained from the experience you learn about yourself.

Bruce brings out the reality that running a marathon is life in a capsule from beginning to end, including the values of early patience and keeping faith to the end. It is your choice to succeed or fail.

If you've already run a marathon, this book will enlighten and widen your understanding of what you have really accomplished. If you've never run a marathon, this book will impart to you an understanding of the task before it has begun. But the real experience can only come from the run itself.

Harold Tinsley
Huntsville, AL

Harold Tinsley is a past president of the Road Runners Club of America and a member of the Hall of Fame. He is also race director of the Rocket City Marathon, held each year in Huntsville.

26.2
Trail of Truth

Let it happen.
Allow.
Run easy.
Life is fun.
But, it's a marathon.

Mile 1

A game. Life's game. The first step.

That moment when competition starts — to conclude with a winner, the one who is first, the one acclaimed.

But is it not also victory to finish, to win within, to know enjoyment so personal that its satisfaction is yours alone?

Life is the alphabet. A to Z. 26 letters. 26 miles. And a little more. Those precious breaths near the finish, something which urges you a little farther, the final 385 yards of life.

Life is the marathon, an enduring race of milestones, young at the start, aging as we seek our destiny, knowing there is finality, and each seeking our own justifications, asking the same questions, each wanting to contribute, each knowing there are many victories needed along this road and that achievement comes to those who stay, who run the full distance, though we may never learn the answer to why am I here, knowing well we will learn the answer to when is the finish?

As there is always a finish, there is also a start. A beginning of the long road that will reveal who and what we are.

Mile one. The course lies ahead. How will I do? How good are the others? Feet pawing, groping, energy to be used, challenges to be met. There will be learning ... thrusting, pushing, surging, testing. They are the challengers, those who seek to be first, to lead, to win, to see how good they can be. Your spirit will be on trial this day.

And some will play the game with cunning, conserving for their moment in this long run of life, watching the front-runner, staying within reach, hoping to be the interloper at the faltering instance.

And some will not compete with the leaders, yet who may be leaders by the way they run this race. They will reason and solve and contribute. They will not be first or last but they, too, will be winners.

And the cautious. Those who run to finish, to whom winning is calculated in personal esteem, good health and long life. They will last, and they will have the time to be themselves, living with enjoyment, blessing as they are blessed.

With the early steps of this marathon there is excitement and concern and wonderment kindled within those embarking, as if on a grand journey, and there is shallow breathing, rapid pulse with the beginning surge. We will discover our abilities and learn that pace is vital in life's race.

To begin the marathon is to feel the strength of youth, knowing there is much reserve, knowing speed and strength, but the wise know speed saps and strength wanes. For the first portion of life's run has vitality, an almost limitless momentum. It will be needed to experiment and discover.

But the pace will level and become the same as you head toward accomplishment's first marker, the first test easy as you stride to the finish of mile one.

Mile 2

Beware.

Energy wasted early can never be reclaimed, for this run is paced survival, a race against yourself.

Can your body maintain this pace? Set the gear and allow controlled enjoyment for this is a decision which must last, a determination of what you will accomplish. A misjudgment and the suffering will bring recall of that decision.

There are others in this living space and only a few will run your pace. Some will be faster, some slower, but there must always be someone who finishes first and another who is last. If you are wise, you will find satisfaction at the end of this long road, for long life is the reward of wisdom exercised.

This is still part of the beginning. Just what have you learned from the first mile? Are you listening? Have you calculated correctly or are you tempted to alter that decision? Do not. It is not the moment to make a serious adjustment. If your pace is too slow or too fast, make a mild change. Allow life to be gentle, treat yourself kindly. The tests will come soon enough.

Steady steps, sure strides are needed now, steps over and over and over and over, seemingly meaningless but which are a measured portion of the total design from point to finish of this scheme, a plan to avoid self-execution and win. The victor and the loser play this game but the choice of awards will be life's joyful hurt or death's pain.

There is some unsteadiness in this second mile, a part of life which must be controlled if you are to benefit from the full measure of this great trial, a drama which will test your physical and mental courage. It is not easy to know the importance of the decision at this early stage. Like childbirth, the pain will not be fully remembered, thus the wise self-counsel heeds self now, smiles later.

As your gentle struggle for control abates, you become self-regulated, automated ... step, step, step, and thoughts

wander, seeking meaningful images to occupy your mind, allowing time to dissipate. Lost time, lost distance. Nearer the goal of getting from one point to another for a particular reason. Know that reason, establish its importance, then allow yourself to attain it.

You have a long span ahead. How you cover the distance will determine the very quality of life, for if you struggle you will be distressed, if you fight you may lose, for this is war, a war within that can only be won by control. Lose control and you will be defeated, a dejected zombie walking the road, but lifeless.

Hold back a little, know you are going to suffer. Your time will be determined not by how you perform in the first few miles, for this is a decision for the long run, a test of how to control yourself, a learning process.

The time for experimenting will be another run, another time, when greater mental toughness is mastered, when you have learned greater control of your will and its ability to have the brain signal as you wish. Keep it simple. You will win if you allow it.

Mile 3

Coast.

You're regulated now and passing time is important. There are times to coast in life, to drift, to just put in miles, float, enjoy.

It is that time. A time to share with others, feel forgotten, breathing without labor, bodies floating through space as participants forget their moments on this stage. It is best not to feel, just be, just perform, just ride the train together and ignore reality.

These early miles are just preparatory, important as a part of the whole but meaningless at the moment. Talk of other days, of tomorrow, stride without knowing, it is time to meander, to speak of other things. Talk of shoes and other runs, take notice of those about you, exchange greetings. Be not serious. Your time will come. Each will recognize it and be born again.

And know the silence within you, an understanding calmness, and hear the sounds of cushioned feet touching the ground and thrusting and touching again and again. There are variations. A touch of the forefoot and so light, so light that touch, speed in those legs. And the mid-foot strike, almost flat, feet shuffling so close to the ground. And the crunch of the heel-striker, pounding, pounding.

You must be midway through this mile. Life has many half-way points, each important because it is the top of a hill and it's down whichever way you go. It's as far or as close to the next milestone as to the last, far or close depending on your state of mind. Goals are always easier when you are strong but the true test is attaining when it is difficult, attaining what most cannot reach. Just the seeking can be difficult, getting there all the more difficult, but oh the joy of the final steps.

This is not man against man, this race. It's not even a race. It's overcoming yourself, defeating yourself, pulling yourself up from negative attitude and procrastination to a more

divine self, a rising up. The mantle of the marathoner is esteemed satisfaction, a knowing glowing of the spirit, a smile that speaks without words.

But you will not know yourself, cannot confront yourself until these early miles and more are done, and every glance and word gets you closer. Seams across the road, mailboxes, a child's waving hand, shadows on the pavement, and someone offers water. Paper cups on the road, the clunk, clunk of other cups dropping, and you notice how quickly the road passes when you look straight down, and you get a little dizzy.

Like irregulars strung out along the road, the column proceeds, some headed toward the unknown, others testing once again. Each wondering. Such is the way for soldiers entering battle, not knowing whether they will make it through.

Ahead is a sign on the road. Just 23 to go, someone says. It snaps your thoughts back to where you are, a body passing through space one step at a time. Not floating, not even gentle. Plodding, striking, breathing, the familiar and ordinary feel and sound. But you will make it, you will make it. You are fine. This is easy so far. Just be patient. A long way to go. A long way.

Check your watch. On schedule, a few seconds fast. No problem, you'll probably slow a little ... just don't strain. Relax, enjoy, this is a special time, remember it...and be strong.

Mile 4

Devilish, feeling great, confident.

And why not, it's going so well. Sure, there's far to go but this is such an easy pace, no need to worry about the oxygen debt of the short run. There are times in life when false confidence is a dangerous guide but surely something that feels so good must be right.

Prancing a few steps, knees lifted higher than normal as if to loosen the legs a bit, you want to laugh aloud but a warning chirps within your brain and you return to a normal stride and ask a running partner, "How ya feelin'?" The partner, equally fresh, replies simply: "Great."

The marathon seems simple, perhaps. Just 13 miles out and 13 miles back, and then the short finish, but that simple logic can turn to terror as many runners become encapsulated in pain that is surely akin to dying, but in the first fourth of life there is much spirit, much energy, much to control.

Feeling great is good and is there any advantage in keeping the notes close to the middle of the scale in order to control the tempo? Will a loss result later from too much happiness so that your feelings tumble a greater distance? Will emotional rise and fall curtail performance? Will control reduce enjoyment, limiting joy but decreasing pain? In the long run, what is best? There will be many such decisions from this point in life and with each mile of experience you will learn that which is better for you.

The bedevilment of this moment is a giddiness seeking enjoyment and what harm is there in laughter? And why not run backwards for a few strides? The energy will drain on this run, to be sure, but the distance must be covered and what good to suffer plodding boredom? The leaders are serious, counting every step, taking the shortest path at every turn. An exact science of the fewest steps possible, utilizing the least energy, machines blending oxygen and fuel with efficiently controlled carburetors.

There are plenty of runners about, all anxious to pass through this space, to sail with unrecognized energy. Like the unseen wind, maybe the mind won't recognize the body's loss and the movement is without energy. Ignored, unnoticed distance can add to the goodness of this passing, for the pleasure of realizing one is farther along than believed equates to a quantum step and a welcomed spurt of spirit.

The flow is in motion, the course sure, attainment will occur, and well there may be pain in this life but there will be joy along the course, joy which must be sampled if there is to be pleasure, and if no pleasure is there life?

It's cool, or warm, or cold, or windy, or drizzling, and someone talks about it, and someone comments, and someone complains, and someone runs best in this weather, and you wonder if the pace is right and search ahead for the mile marker. It's there, just ahead, and you watch the incessantly changing numbers on the watch as you reach mile four with a smile.

Just a jaunt...and didn't that mile go quickly?

Mile 5

Every step is easy this early in the race, the pace established, no pain, just easing along.

A feeling of haughtiness, confidence. The fraction game begins. Nearly one-sixth of the way with the four-mile marker strides behind and forgotten. Keep looking ahead and float. Just float. Touch the ground lightly. And smile. There will be plenty of time later for hurting. It's a time of happiness, excitement, and with each step you glide toward a finish line destiny, there to accomplish what few have ever done.

Compute the time. Were you on pace at the fourth mile? If this pace is maintained, what will be the finish time? Keep computing, it passes time.

The pavement slopes gradually upward and the ascent begins with measured steps. Just maintain the pace, don't push, don't waste energy, don't fight, don't lean too much, just maintain. How will any hill feel late in the race?

It's early in this lifespan, still learning. It's a challenge just to be, to pass through space unfeeling, a near non-existence.

Gravity tugs as muscles thrust, legs pump, feet thump, arms drive, the crest ahead, just ahead. Just a challenge, early stress, a test met.

Gently down, a pleasure. For every uphill in life, there is an equal downhill somewhere, sometime, an easing, a respite, a break, a time to cruise. Easy, just plopping along. Pace, pace, pace, mustn't rush as there's a long way to go. Being steady has its significance in life. There are times to maintain a steady course; there will be plenty of challenge later.

Just lope, let everything be easy. It is a time to enjoy, to feel. It is not yet a race, it is a time for growing and learning and experiencing, and passing time without suffering, thinking as little as possible of the moment, wandering on wayward beams.

A bird flutters. Seize the moment and watch it race skyward. A few yards without thought.

It is a game of the mind, this marathon. A game of gentle compulsion, seeking anything but concern, anything that will fool the brain, as if not realizing equates to movement without energy, and perhaps it does. But what matter, the time is lost and that is good. It would be difficult to count every step, measure every moment, for sanity requires moments when we only look into space, gazing at anything or nothing at all.

It is an adventure with space, just being, just filling these moments, just quiet movement like a ship on its course, the port of departure forgotten, destination unseen over an endless horizon.

There is also reality, the ability to focus on the moment and determine circumstances before deciding what next. The reality is the fifth mile marker. The finish is just 21 miles, 385 yards away. Unlike life, we know the exact end of this race and, once finished, we will be stronger for the next, for will is might and with will comes accomplishment, with might comes victory.

Mile 6

For every passing mile there is challenge.

It's you against yourself, but do not fight, less you be defeated. Rather, allow yourself to succeed, testing and growing, constantly testing.

It's like any of life's improvements. To improve, you must learn who you are and eliminate limitations, for there are no limits other than those imposed by yourself. Allow limits to dissipate. Be gentle, but grow, enjoy and know yourself, then allow growth by testing and let yourself run a little better, longer. You may be surprised that growth will sometimes be larger than anticipated, but you allowed it to be so.

The mature runner might better understand this because of life's experiences. You learn from sorrow and elation that to survive you must control emotions within manageable levels. It's a very certain mental toughness required in life that can be developed from running. What greater daily test than mentally maneuvering while running — challenging, enjoying, pushing, questioning, relaxing, escaping, playing, hurting, then thrusting onward to where only discoverers can go. It is an enjoyable hurt.

It is knowing, a knowing that the accomplishment is personal, that what you feel is yours alone, something another can realize only in the doing.

Your life, this marathon, is especially important to only one being, the one who's going to hurt, the one who must strengthen that side of the thought process that says "you can do it." It's not easy to defeat that little Satan who sits on one shoulder and suggests the pain isn't worth it, but you can, and the pride of knowing what you suffer for that victory is yours alone. Others will listen but only you will know its measure.

Somewhere in this mile you will be one-fifth complete, about the middle of March in our human calendar, and what lies ahead is defeat and victory. What greater attainment

than to defeat your former self, to create a new-and-better person, thereby winning by defeating.

A foot touches the ground and lifts as the other swings ahead to grasp new ground. One step ahead, and another; it is a constancy you learn, that you will prevail, that finishing really is winning, that the victor must last the contest.

Ahead is a curve, a bend, but when such are added to the straight lines and the ups and downs it all averages out. We travel the same distance together. There will be curves and hills, and life itself can be an obstacle if you allow it to be.

It is in knowing that you smile and continue the solitary steps that added together will equal more than the total, for what is the sum of learning plus achievement?

Mile 7

Give of yourself in measured dosage.

Partake of water but keep moving. A ritual predetermined, a part to be played, elixir needed by the body and that greater you.

This life nearly one fourth complete. Two more 10Ks and you will discover the more difficult final quarter and suffer what will seem to be the last half. Measure and maintain, comfortably, gently gaining on others. It is not a time to race.

That others are ahead matters little. It will always be so, but everyone is diminished during this span and you will gain with prudence, patience, for it is the story of life itself — you are born and grow and take the place of others who gained in another moment of time.

Your moment is now. It is yours alone. How you perform pulses from inner awareness, a rhythm, which under control will take you across the expanse to truth, to the summation of a trial in which your peers may judge but only you will know, wisdom earned of restraint.

Another runner has another presence and has little significance to you. He in his moment, you in yours. That he charges ahead is his test.

Drift under control. Light touches, tender moments, sailing just above the pavement. Ecstasy, meditative, lost but on course.

Why do you run this marathon? To attain? And will your smile be greater, gaze higher? Will many small steps equate to quantum stride? Will your being evolve through some certainty, some assuredness, some quiet truth?

Will others recognize a new person, one more sure, yet change not obvious? There are such transformations in life when a person seems more vibrant, when others become more aware of your presence, sense leadership, seek answers, and you are elevated to a new level without effort.

Your body is functioning well at the end of this seventh mile, sweat flowing, muscle fuel depleting gradually as you glide past a slowing figure. Efficiency is required on the long run and you have envisioned this run mile by mile, imagery that conditioned the brain.

You can do it.

You will.

You must.

Mile 8

How you perceive yourself is who you are.

It is in believing that greatness is allowed, knowing you will accomplish, staring challenge in the eye and prevailing, lifting, lifting, soaring determinedly, daringly, defiantly, driving ever onward to where others only dream.

Such self-belief is the marathoner's perception. Skill and will, training and determination, the ability to run farther, faster.

It is flight with Orville and Wilbur, the run of Phidippides, the Tank Corps of Patton, men whose perceptions became mortal energy and reality.

And who are you at this point in the race? Steadfast. A pawn on a self-controlled board, planned movement in preparation for the later challenges of this game, challenges that will require focus and will, challenges which must be defeated through controlled thought and movement.

On and on, stride and stride and stride and stride, occupy moments, allow enjoyment, a gentleness defying measurement, and thoughts focus on pace and there is no answer to how you feel. You just are.

Life has times like this, just existing, lasting, doing, knowing with each Monday there is a Friday ahead, that living is often small steps, but with each day's accomplishment there is gain. Every life is a marathon, and those about you will gain from knowing your strength and will lead others.

Winning is in finishing, lasting the full distance. A man who quietly stays the course, whose attainments are realized through sweat, contributes much and gains admiration though he need not recognize it.

Constancy is strength.

Others are ahead, others behind, you will finish, some will not. There is much difference between believing and trying, knowing and hoping, and you will often try and hope in life and there will be difficulties, but with each difficult moment comes opportunity and with each trying event

comes learning. Pause often but always remember those experiences and keep going, for trying and hoping will become believing and knowing.

Winning comes with time.

Mile 9

It is a precarious edge.

To run this finely tuned engine so it propels you at just the right speed for exactly 26 miles, 385 yards, to expend energy efficiently so the fuel lasts the distance while you test the limits of endurance.

Oh, it is a fine edge.

You will meet a gaunt figure resembling death and it will be you, screaming within yourself, essence draining, body dying, and you know it is out there, but still you move onward.

Before this mile is complete, you will have reached the one-third point and there is some comfort in that. Assuredly no feeling of dread; there is little feeling, a trance allows little excitement or disappointment. You just pass through this space at a predetermined pace, always steady, attuned to this body, listening, calculating, and step, step, stepping as gently as possible, if only imagined, for if it is imagined it is real, for that is part of the marathon, these mind games that occupy space and keep away suffering.

Easy, easy, easy strides, arms swinging gently, a glistening body slices through the early morning stillness, eyes surveying the long road and you don't wonder how much farther. You know the thought hangs suspended but you won't allow it, and because you don't think it, there is less concern.

Onward, onward to that meeting with your gaunt self.

A bird speeds from a tree and to another, followed by a flitting pursuer, a momentary distraction. Enjoy the moment, for time passeth with diversion, unthought time lost forever.

And a pickup truck roars past with youthful voices shouting. It is a part of running — the jeers are admiration and you wonder if the shouters realize it, and you are pleased to have realized this truth.

Thoughts are clear; you often solve problems on long runs as body and brain relate, and you know that today something greater than either will be needed to succeed.

There's still a long way to go.

Mile 10

Just 17 miles, 385 yards to go.

With nine miles completed, you're more than one-third done. There's much exploring ahead.

Squeezing the cup of water, you bend the top inward so it is small enough to fit entirely in your mouth so you can consume its contents without spilling. By counting the cups along the road you estimate how many runners are ahead.

It's not important.

Some of the runners are drifting back to you, struggling a little, backing off the pace. Are you running too fast? No, right on schedule, maybe a little slow ... just not fast. That would be a mistake. Got to stay on pace.

A hill lies ahead, challenging. "Maintain, use the same energy, don't back off." The thought streams across your consciousness, almost without effort, and the roads begins to lift as you lean gently into the hill, pushing, pushing, arm swing accentuated, and you retain the rhythm. Cresting at the top, the same effort quickens the stride that is to be kept despite labored breathing. The strain will subside. A short distance, a smile, all's normal, just a bump in life.

The road cuts, twisting to the right, and a sharp downhill to the left, then a series of rolling hills, a roller coaster diversion. It all evens out, ups and downs are part of the whole. It is the "in between" of every start and finish that challenges, taunts, tests. Everyone can start but it is that vast division between beginning and end which determines achievement. With the finish in sight, the sprint can be accomplished, but getting there — that is the greater.

The middle ground can be vast, if permitted to be, for with worry and fear the distance is greater, with smile and joy lesser. Is then the distance traveled the same?

Enjoy the spirit which propels you, feel the lightness of your movement, witness all that is about you, and go with joyful determination, knowing, enjoying, for that which comes will be and all that is, is.

RED LOBSTER
10K CLASSIC
3064

Pain is real but is recognized as part of this passing, for it is part of this wondrous experience, needed for attainment, the expectation a reality of this noble journey. Without the richness of suffering, there is less fulfillment, less achievement. Is it not meaningful to suffer to attain, to win within by sustaining?

Mile 11

Knowing yourself.

Pacing, feeling, controlling ...

Big league stuff, this marathon, attainable only through reasoned determination. The skill the ability to know how fast to allow this body to be driven; reasoned knowing a learned skill from a brain trained by a constantly tested body. Balance is the answer of this moment. Just go.

Each mile a part of this play, life staged mile to mile, the actor naked unto himself, clothed only with resoluteness, a purposeful control his only garment. But it is much, it is all, and onward goes the pilgrim in search of his grail.

All that is is now, the single step of the thousands which lie ahead, each subtracting minutely, a runner staying the course, entranced in infinite present moments leading to the ultimate attainment. Time is always now, movement is always now, triumph will be felt now. Time is not an enemy, we merely set a course of ongoing moments to reach a destination, which will always be present when attained.

The enemy is within, but therein is also strength, strength honed by countless miles, messages related incessantly to the brain from endless striding, physical being and mental presence entwined in a compact that will not, cannot, be forgotten. But uncertainty will be with you always, a question that will haunt through life. It must be dashed by an overriding strength, but the swordsman must await his weakness and it is too soon.

Mind dull, inattentive, as if entranced, molecules swoosh around this human projectile moving steadily along a tar road. A tin-roofed house unseen as a marathoner moves through life unknowing; there are times when thought process is not needed, a person occupying space, taking the present with him as he goes from where he began to where he will be.

Thousands of todays will be experienced; it is living, feeling, enjoying, hurting, laughing. Others will share much

of that, but not this moment, not your moments, for this is private, this is getting there. This is you.

Suffer now for tomorrow's present moment, knowing satisfaction will be the bliss of the wiser, if older, you.

On, on, on, a mortal ticking, steady beat, beat, beating of a heart pump, pump, pumping, breath steady, a runner transfixed.

A little girl watches from her front yard, a slender athlete in shorts and running shoes glides past.

She watches in wonderment, a curiosity, perhaps with profound effect, receiving an unknown contribution, that which we all give, for each of us are parts of many.

Still more runners appear and the little girl calls out, "How far are you running?"

"A marathon."

("How far is that?", she wonders, believing it must be very far.)

Mile 12

Lope.

Graceful, a frivolous flow, an antelope bouncing playfully over the prairie, a cheerful spirit, a soaring bird using the current of wind for propulsion.

A waltz, a minuet, a melding of muscle and drifting, sweat and inner sounds a partnership of dance and music, strains of a favored song occupy thought and subvert time.

Onward the body, savored passage, enjoyment a portion of every day — and this is a special day, one of challenge, growth, testing of your quality. You will speak often to your inner self on this day and there will be a struggle for control.

But, a warning: Let not comfort be your master. The water you drink will only quench temporarily, there is a life thirst this day which will be quenched only at the finish.

Your body fuel will deplete, the gauge going from full to empty, but there is a fulfilling gift at the conclusion of this race — one you give yourself. It will affect all you touch.

We all give to each other, imitate traits, take from each other, become a part of each other. We owe a debt to mankind. Today you will prove yourself and will touch more lives tomorrow with new inner strength.

A certainty, a knowing, a winged man, but be not alone for you are to hug all creatures, sharing your soul and strength and smile with embrace, a silent message of comfort which affirms friendship. And remember this for all the days ahead for we are all tested in every mile of our mortal existence and what you share today will be passed to some other being along this path — and all shall be the greater and every affection shall multiply and the sum far greater than the total of innocent clasps, for purity is virtue and in the opening of spirit the shield is released.

And you must also receive, for to only give is to deprive others of their gifts, which must also be given.

Share by giving and receiving, and the measure matters not except that it be continuous and with good spirit. If

your plate is full, you have too much. The bread may be shared. And if you are in pain, let another administer. Bread for comfort is good. But if you are not in pain and still you give bread, you soothe one's hunger who may offer comfort to another. And, still, you have received.

Whether we hobble or run, we share passage with the pain and joy of those who trek with heavy load up a mountain trail or lope gently along the meandering valley road amid lush green and the view of the mountains.

There are many steps toward the sunset of each day and with the morrow comes new light and troubled skies with clouds of puffed white and black laced with a jagged streak of yellow ... and you run with determination along the trail through the valley and wind around the rocks of a mountain road and push toward your summit.

It is good just to be.

Mile 13

Measure carefully.

A dozen mile markers have passed and your body anticipates the half-way point. It is a time for caution, for it would be easy to let go, to pick up the pace, to move more quickly to complete the first half of this run.

Measure well; the house glass runneth.

Know the second half will be the same distance, yet longer. Though the steps may be of same count, pain and doubt will make it farther.

Be joyful, let this distance pass playfully, smiling as you prance. There is less enjoyment ahead.

Thrust without effort, slide gently through this space, it is only a part of the whole, merely adding to the sum, this half consumed easily, but it is the portion which follows that is the more difficult, for it is you who are consumed slowly, ever slowly, evenly and efficiently.

Finishing this half is fun, spirited, the mid point in life; wisdom will be gained from the time which is left. There are many sunsets, an equal number of dawns, when seeds are planted a harvest follows.

As the spring flower knows its time, to bloom early is to risk death, but the marathoner's demise is a curse full of pain, slow pain, dying with each step, but he will not die. He cannot.

The marathoner must live to finish.

Ease onward lofty flight, be aglow. Time's testing is about to begin, that time which claws, reaches out to pull us from our destination and which will devour the undetermined.

But there is a choppy water to be gentled, a calming lake within us that when tamed allows floating flight, and these final steps through the seeming timelessness of the first half are nearing completion; it is the second half of life when time is ever more meaningful, when wisdom is matched with enduring. Youth allows running the wide curve, age takes the wiser course.

Conservation is preservation, seeking to maintain youth but knowing if you are to be young on this day you must also be wise. It is the 12th hour, the inner clock ticking ceaselessly, the pendulum swinging gently from side to side encased in a sleek body, its face in a steady gaze ignoring its inner workings but the hands move in a steady sequence, responding to the conductor of this symphony of notes moving across the score of this day.

And the ticking seems louder, louder, the mile marker appears and you sense the midday hour is to be announced, the 12th hour reached, the 13th mile on today's clock, but time will not determine whether you finish this day. You will finish. It's the distance, the distance, and so the challenge begins, the truest test of all.

To beat pain and inner doubts and defeat yourself. To overcome, to outlast, to finish. To win.

Mile 14

Now!

The race begins, the diminishing body silently surrendering of itself without warning signals to its controller.

The race is to outlast.

Relaxing caution, you quicken, the challenge is on. Runner versus his being, his thoughts. The irony is the runner must befriend, yet control, both — knowing each may betray.

A shadow skims along the tar, a silhouette shortening, bumping, lengthening with the indentations of the byway, accompanying a runner on a path to destiny.

You can direct your own course in life, determine the banks of your river, but today you must prove your ability to also follow a planned course of action, proving ability to accomplish.

Design. Your plan a preconceived vision of every mile; you've run this race in your mind, training your brain. You know when to loosen, you alone hold the reigns on this trotter, maintaining, maintaining, perhaps prancing spiritedly awhile but parameters kept with a smile.

On and on goes the conqueror, scantily clad but this battle does not require full raimant, indeed a single ounce pounded to the pavement many thousands of times is heavy weight indeed, draining mortal strength from this warrior.

Body glistening, breathing unhampered, muscles working in harmony with nerve-transmitted messages from the brain, sinew and bone providing structure, absorbing the shock of relentless jolts, heels and toes and knees and hips transmitting feelings which are received and analyzed without effect, arms sliding forward and back like an old steam engine turning its wheels, the courier Phidippides running to Sparta before the battle of Marathon, an effort of valor being replicated on this route of honor.

Moving methodically, you determine to alter your pace a little and begin to move up on the runner some 20 yards

in front. It must be a gradual move for there is far to go and energy cannot be expended foolishly and once having caught that runner you will feel compelled to remain ahead. The lesson is important, to be patient, to stalk with cautioned determination.

As you move closer, you know this is a diversion and a challenge. Something different to give some diversity, to alter thinking, provide relief through some slight variety, but you are also challenging another runner, who may not want to be passed.

As you approach you quicken slightly to show strength, gliding by in rhythm, form strong, and the other runner says, "Looking good...", and you reply, "Hang in there." And maintaining the slightly faster pace until you feel securely ahead, a doubt slips into your thoughts. Have you picked up the pace too much? Will you regret this much later in the race?

No, you're fine. Dismiss the negative thoughts; they are destructive. Think positive, less stress, much better because you won't be fighting yourself. Mind and body need to be together for the difficult road.

Mile 15

Onward.

Onward to where others only dream, untamed, spirited, flowing with sweat, loving this time, this place, heady and giddy, galloping these furlongs toward the richest purse ever — to finish a marathon, to be among the small percentage of mankind who ever ran the distance.

A driven runner, arms swinging, passing through on the way to glory.

The toughest standard of all is self-measurement. Doubting your own abilities, doubt assuaged only by knowledge — and knowledge comes with the many steps in life. The only absolute is occurrence, for only with experiencing anything does it truly become a part of you — and repetition becomes memory and memory knowledge, but what is gained can be dulled by time and uncertainly will reappear.

Repetitive steps of this marathon etch within the brain and is filed through the membrane of the subconscious, and you will know attainment of the impossible for some is probable for you.

For although the marathon is akin to birth, the pain of experiencing life, and even the feeling of dying on this day, shall enrich you beyond today's finish line. As we are living each day, so, too, are we closer to dying, but the marathon provides an insight to death as the body consumes itself, depletes, drains ...

Onward! Onward to where others only dream, slash stoically ever onward. Pursuing the dream is what alone brings the answers to the eternal, unending search for whatever it is that drives those few on to the rim of breakthrough.

It is that pursuit which broke the four-minute barrier in the one-mile run, that which sleeplessly forces the scientist through hours and days and weeks and years of testing and retesting and starting over again to solve a riddle and offer the cure.

If you can finish the marathon, what else can you do? What else can't you do? Finishing the marathon is mental domination of the physical self; it is also dominion over thought, a conscious force that overrides objections fielded by the brain.

You are beginning to hurt a little but you keep pushing, you don't have room for hurt, don't have time to be concerned about it. Moving, foot, foot, foot touching, thrusting, legs lifting and foot driving downward again, an unending mechanical movement that will not cease until the road ends. It is the day of totality, a culmination of weeks of training and thought, and this race belong to you, the explorer, the conqueror.

Waving hands and encouraging words greet your senses and you wave and smile. "Thank you," you say. And there's music ahead and children yelling and a table with water. Encouragement, refreshment, all needed from this way station.

And such it is. When help is needed, keep going. It will be there.

Mile 16

P<small>ace.</small>

Winners set standards, determined efforts, reasoned tenets for others to follow. The pacer wills, it matters not that others will follow.

The pacer is not a leader, he is beyond that station, for the notes were placed on the score in order to play this song note by note. It is a precise melody that only the pacer knows, a personal metronome which accommodates the conductor.

Paced steps, air gasped by hungering lungs, arms and legs in unison, blood pumped along its own precise course.

We do know our purpose in this life. It is to finish. Ever you seek your own destination, moving along a predestined path, measuring, seeking, hurting, achieving.

Eternally we flow along the musical score, scaling up, drifting down, but with each note the movement continues.

Doubt is ever present but like the metronome beating incessantly, you keep going, energy depleting like granules of sand flowing in the hourglass. But unlike the measurement of time, only distance is certain in the marathon.

Pace must be so precise that the finish is reached as the last granules are falling.

Knowing when you reach the 16-mile marker, there will be just 10 miles left – a distance you have run many times, there is anticipation, a hope of getting to that point as soon as possible, but you will get there when you get there. No sooner. The pace must be held.

Anticipation can be a fearful feeling. It is that which children suffer when they want tomorrow to come, when excitement is nearly too much. The marathoner can't afford it, the best feelings a dull mind, a wandering mind, a problem-solving mind, pleasant thoughts, or no thoughts. Anything to keep from thinking a lot about the marathon.

The sound of breath, listening to the inhaling and exhaling sounds, is about all the excitement this runner wants.

Listen often to yourself, be attuned, aware, because to know yourself is to to like yourself, and if you are to improve isn't it better to begin by best knowing the soul that inhabits this body? And, by listening to your physical body, you will sense illness and better be prepared for it, likely even avoid it. Habits, weaknesses, fears and more can be defeated.

Holding the arm up to check the time on the watch, you determine you are right on schedule and mile 16 is about 30 seconds ahead. From that point on, you'll be on your normal Sunday run. You try not to think that you've already run 16 miles.

No problems, no problems, feeling okay, a little tired, not going to hit the wall, you're going to make it because there's just 10 to go. The real countdown in underway — for this race, for the rest of your life.

Mile 17

Questioning.

Without questions, can there be answers? Without wonderment, fulfillment? Without doubt, the full measure of satisfaction that is solution?

The road is long, this road is long, but repetitive steps shorten its length. You are constantly nearer attainment, no matter the tiny waves of doubt which rise, which ebb, the logic cannot be disputed — you are always nearer finishing.

One man, courageous, alone, will complete this adventure, conquering his mortal inner self, pressing through doubts, bringing forth strength from inner depth to examination, testing and creating a new being.

Questions, yes there are questions. Can I do it? Will I make it?

And there will always be an answer, but the answer you desire comes only from demand of self, resolute fortitude, a refusal to give any but the required answer.

You will finish if you have to crawl. In times of great need, it is the only way, finishing being the only possibility allowed. The questions bring a demanding, determined dose of force. Force that drives, force that conquers, that which overrides opposition, a tank rumbling over open land, retreating warriors in flight.

Pounding, pounding, heels striking, forefoot thrusting, thighs and calves operating in sequence as legs lift and reach, and applauding hands encourage, hands clapped together by those along the way, shouted sounds encourage, a cowbell, familiar music, and you remember a truth — you win from within.

Victory is most complete when you have been tested and from somewhere within your response is "Win!" Like a great flash loosened across the sky, a rumble begins, and rolls, and is unleashed.

Response. Will. Win.

And with clinched fist you flail the air, striking mightily outward like a pitcher ripping a high, fast ball past a helpless batsman.

You are unbeatable.

Mile 18

Reality.

The hill.

There are many hills, some long, some steep, all real. But the finish is not at the top. You must go beyond, this is the marathon. The finish beyond the last measured mile, at the other side of this hill and more.

The hill.

Gotta do it, gotta do it, determined gain. The greater the difficulty, the greater the satisfaction later, it's just that reality is now, the pain real. Memory of pain doesn't hurt but satisfaction of accomplishment lasts as long as memory.

Life is fair. To the top tough, and the pace over the top must be held, but effort has reward and for each up there is down. There will always be some hills and to be able to scale them is its own reward. Some cannot even walk.

Gotta do it. Lean, push, gotta do it, you must. You know you can, you know you can, you have, you will, thrust! With breath charging from your body, gasping in new air, you fight to maintain pace. Don't back off, breathing will soon be normal, and you reach the top.

The downhill flight is to be enjoyed — not fought, a sailing, fanciful rush, a joyful striding from cloud to mist, floating from a star to reality. Flying without effort, winged soaring, gliding, riding on your own feet, a quickened pace without determination.

From severe pain has come relative joy. It is often true that to attain there must be pain but do not fight yourself. Allow good things to happen, for in allowing there is natural gentleness, in forcing there is always pain. Choose your moments but do not back away from necessary challenge.

Halfway down the hill, there is a quick rise; It is a moment of pause, mental refueling, allowing the body a brief rest before hurtling downward without thought. It is needed in your race, for as we work, so too must we rest.

And the road goes downward again . You cannot control many circumstances but with each such moment there is opportunity. You lean slightly forward and gain momentum. Know there is good in nearly all circumstances and develop the ability to be able to take advantage of them.

But patient, patient must you be as you span this moment, then again taking command, seeking another wind as captain of your ship, never to return to the passed moment.

And over the distant horizon you disappear from those who watch — you were a part of their moment and now gone, for your moment is forever, though you share the path.

Mile 19

Steadfast.

To stay the course with resoluteness, being devoted to worthwhile purpose like love, dependability, honor, purity, begins with self-honesty, and for what else do you run the marathon but to know yourself and remove limitations?

Goodness is within each person but is not always present, but those who give of themselves shall be the richer. Be steadfast in this and all good purpose, for to what end will your finish be dedicated but to yourself? And it is your true self which is confronted on this day, examined, tested, proven.

Straight ahead, continuous, completing this life test with grit. The diligent are rewarded with much, for doesn't constant investment reap compounded returns? This investment will bear interest for the remainder of life. Hold to the course, for goals set must be achieved in order that your life be satisfying through attainment. Success nurtures psyche, that which gives strength which shines through your face as if from a spring releasing clear water to nourish the soul.

Cadence, this march from belief through uncertainty. Cadence, this measured movement from excitement through dullness. Cadence, this two-step harmony played unceasingly through the travail of this passage through nothingness, but the cause, the cause, all meaningful and the script followed like single drum beats in step, step, step.

A muttered complaint, sounding only within, a questioning anguish, but still you maintain, prescribed orders obeyed, an abyss of time, agony too deep for measurement, a runner in the primeval void headed to creation.

Patience is often accompanied by suffering, the will to endure a virtue of perseverance, the solitary runner the very symbol of this personal right to perform with resolute self-control, a forbearing stoicism, an unflinching indif-

ference to pain in order to pass through tedium en route to ultimate conclusion, the fundamental principle sought in this individual contest, no higher victory than to finish, utmost attainment, the final step.

No one else can feel your pain, know your hurt, you alone must conquer, and this conquest only accomplished one step at a time, one foot in front of the other repeated, recurring, continuous, an unending repetition, ceaselessly moving onward. Persisting uninterrupted, an unceasing progression, a tempo of motion, a continuum of multiplied steps, a gait across this span of life.

And what will you attain without constancy? To stop is to lose steps, steps which can only be regained with speed, but in the long run speed will not endure.

On you plod and you know not that the trailing runner has lost ground, you are mute, uncaring, unconcerned, incapable of feeling, knowing only that to continue is to reduce distance and that there are more than seven miles to go.

Mile 20

T rouble.

Why am I doing this? Still so far to go.

Feet heavy, a struggle, the emptiness of hollow hurting, consumption, a body devouring, wasting, perishing, corroding from the inside.

Incredible how we must suffer to receive the fullest measure, the greater sufferer the greater painter, the greater writer. The memory of this unending instant never to be forgotten and the end not in sight.

It is a day of judgment, a day to measure the future, to establish direction, to settle with yourself, to determine whether you rule or exist. Your dead reckoning known by distance and sign, you are precisely in position, and upon finishing you will plot tomorrow.

Trouble is a constant messmate, and an opportunity, as calamity travels the companionway with many sailors, a stairway that goes up as well as down. Seek the deck, feel the breeze, sail the horizon, find what is ahead by eternal pursuit. It is there, it is out there. Encourage others, for there is no end to opportunity, the pot is always full for those who are determined to find it and take of its measure.

Distress is only a signal, an agitation, a vexation seeking cure, an inconvenience that pesters but which brings attention to resolution. Worry brings misfortune or chance, your fate to choose, but greater gold will be attained by drive than by luck, a personification of prosperity wrought by your own will. Better to choose than to lose.

Control force, transport yourself with reason, propel with the vigor needed and no more, achieving purpose, pressing reasonably but with fixed purpose, determining future by your decisions and the will to never quit. The way is long but is always present, thus distance is a partner and a friend.

Surrender never but be wise, yielding a position while continuing onward, conceding but never becoming a

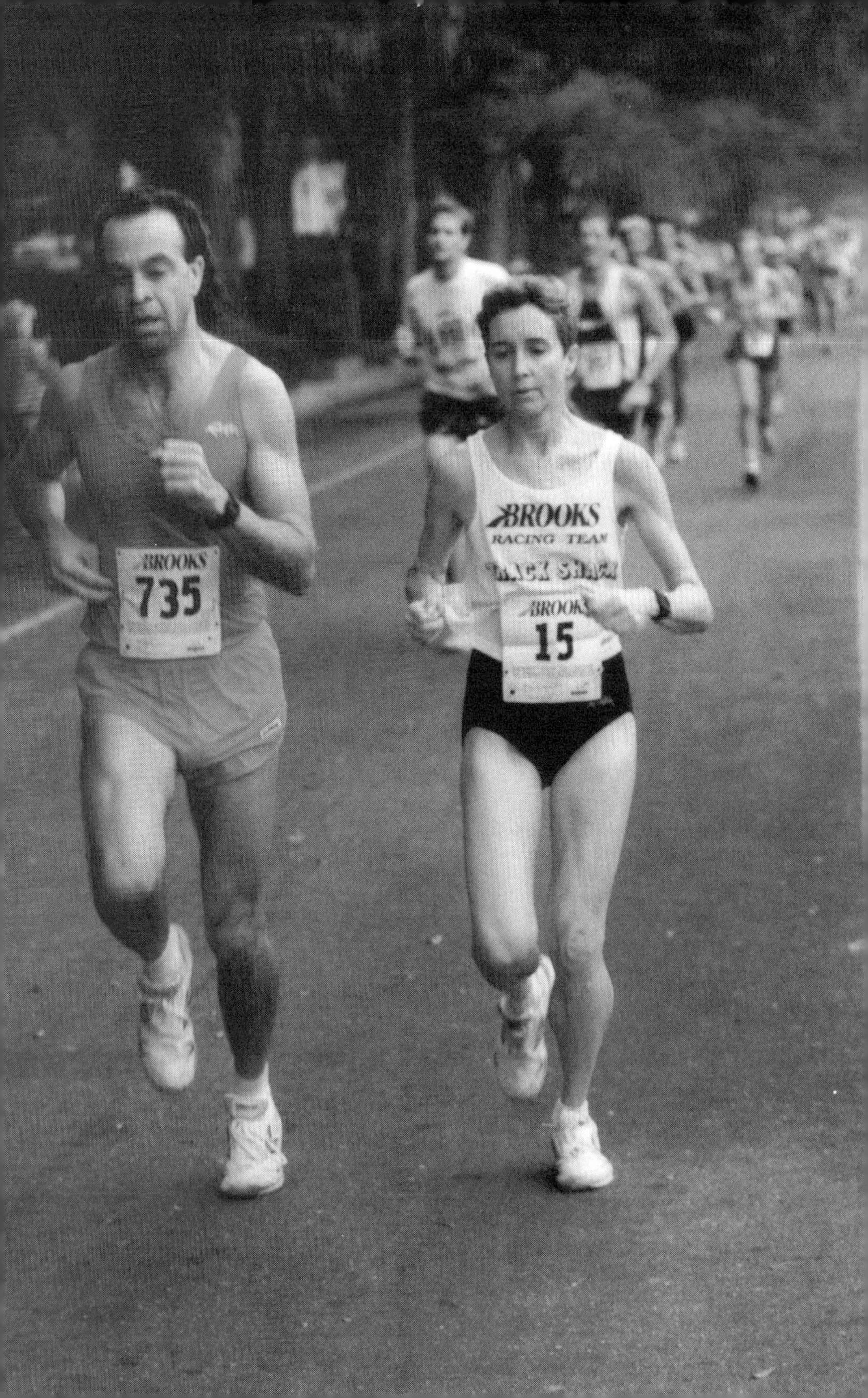
BROOKS
735
BROOKS
RACING TEAM
BROOKS
15

prisoner or abandoning motion to the goal line. The river bends but keeps flowing, rapids impede but do not stop. Even the dam must eventually be opened; do not give up.

And you moan, "I will finish. I will finish if I have to crawl. There is no way I can be stopped, nothing will prevent me from finishing, no matter how bad I feel." And you will finish because you have ordained it. It is vital to you, necessary for you, and it drives you to continue.

Life goes on but the lost moment is gone forever, never to be found, never to be relived, time which cannot be recaptured. Eternity is now and always and endless and you are the forerunner of your own being, preceding your future by preparing the way of your tomorrows, heralding what you are to be, preparing your way down future's road.

For you are, you will be, the sum of what you are today, for tomorrow will be today, and you are always in the present, time always now, never changing, but you can lengthen your time by using more than others, progression with purpose.

Mile 21

Used up, miserable.

Misery the master but overcoming it creates a new ruler.

Last, get through this, keep going, there really is a finish, though miles ahead. Every step closer to the end, absolute truth which cannot be doubted.

Endure, blank mind, a gaunt figure with a stare — a soldier in a line of weary combat troops moving mindlessly to wherever they go, there to regain vitality. Ours is not just to move through space, but there are moments when that is useful. Time lost that is not missed. a time of near-consciousness obeying a command to march.

There is strength in this dullness, a mental trickery, a command from your very soul to alter visual perception, to see and not care, to provide relief by avoiding reality. You are very alone in this blankness, a respite.

"Looking good..."

The clanging of a cowbell, a water stop, and the brain perceives and you return to the present because there was no command to march *and* drink. But, there is one command still certain.

Keep going.

And a breeze wafts across your face as birds fly across the road, one chasing another, and flit into the leaves and branches of a tree, and you smile. Why hurt intolerably when there's beauty everywhere? Birds chirping, wind moving, blue sky with clouds puffing, wild flowers, green trees, and there is beauty of thought and song.

And you allow a tune to drift through your mind. You realize you have exercised control, suggesting, no *allowing*, a particular tune. The greater control you have over your own thought process, the more you can attain and what greater control than to will your body to complete a run of such proportions?

Your smile is the truest form of beauty. That grin changed you and has power to change all others, for the smile is

common to all, a pleasant enjoyment, personal and shared, for one person's smile can alter emotion, allow kindness, open thoughts of kinship, affection, amusement, and create a sparkling of the eyes.

Perhaps the marathon should be 26 smiles and a little more.

Smile within. It helps.

Mile 22

Value this moment.

Just hang on. It is a valuable lesson this marathon teaches, learning to just keep going.

There will be many times when just putting one foot in front of the other is required — to stop an admission of failure, just to keep going avoids defeat and retains the possibility of victory.

You hurt, question, but keep going, strides adding inches and feet and yards and miles, with each step the destination closer.

The final 385 yards possible only with steps taken in the passage of time, for time is ever moving and failure to move with it equals a sure sum:

Failure.

Success is often decided by the amount of time necessary to pass from one point to another. Movement is both time and distance.

A marathon is a precise distance, a space with defined boundaries. Space is time and movement.

You are somewhere between alpha and zeta and it doesn't matter where, only that movement continues.

On, onward on this pilgrimage, destiny each next step. There will be many boundaries to reach and dissolve.

With every step of this mile you are closer, closer, and strength builds with the confidence of knowing you will complete this race.

And you hurt, oh you hurt. Surely this must be the feeling of near-death, for this body is withering, consuming itself, muscles fatigued, steps slower.

Can't collapse, can't stop now, got to keep going.

Mile 23

W ithin.

Alone, you've discovered what courage is, confronted an enemy who cannot be seen, yet which is with you always — within.

It will take determination which equates to valor, to overcome, to outlast, to defeat, to win by constant forward motion, as if horse-mounted, sword drawn, you move constantly forward, slashing, driving the invader to retreat.

It is the only way. To finish is everything, the ultimate triumph, to defeat the one who stands in your way, the soul which when victoriously defied becomes a marching companion, a sword bearer ready for other challenges. The enemy is within; it is you.

A muscle twitches, a cramp, and you reach for your thigh and rub awkwardly, moving, always moving, knowing that finishing results from always moving, but you hobble, walk a few steps, rubbing, jumping with pain, and keep going. The spasm subsides. Peace. And there must be less than four miles to go.

Please, please. Got to finish, will finish.

You quicken the pace, altering, just doing something different, the tempo changed, a variation, time passes. A hundred yards, just a hundred yards from that surge. How many more hundred yards are there? Got to get that out of mind, keep going, keep moving, keep running.

"I may be dying but I won't die until I get to the finish line." A pledge, a damned determination of will. There is no other way. Less than four miles to go. With the next mile marker there will be three miles to go. The last 385 yards don't count. You could crawl that far but you know you'll run it, that strength will come from somewhere within — that same enemy who seeks to subvert can also provide strength, as if surrendering in the final moment with a joyous surge.

The mind is dull now, the body force draining, doggedly you go one step at a time, plodding, plodding, just going, outlasting, seeking to blot our space and time and doubt.

A curve, surely that sign will be around that curve, and with slowed steps the distance to the destination is shortened and ahead a sign does appear. You know exactly how far three miles is. It's the distance from home to the telephone pole just beyond the furniture store, a run you've done many times.

Sure you know it's not the same to run three miles at the end of 23 but it's still the same distance. Yes, it will take longer. Damned truth: Space and time are related.

Mile 24

X.

The crossroads.

About 5,000 meters left, a little over three miles. There are many short distances in our pilgrimage and many crossroads; this one is pivotal.

A decisive jaunt, mental gallop, onward, onward to destiny, a totality of human accomplishment — attaining what few ever attempt. Not just to finish. To prevail.

Savor, the steps still many but the end certain, a rare moment transcending time, space, distance ... infinity. A juncture with another dimension. The cadence ongoing, legs lifting, an awakening of spirit, a perseverance, a lone runner pushes around a bend.

Almost there, a frequent human condition, an encouragement and a realization that it will happen. Almost there, the words take on almost magical proportion and you rejoice with the thought of completion.

There are so many crossroads, so many decisions to be made, and this one was simply just there. A crossroads, to be sure, but you just kept going. You are now in the shortest distance of a normal road race, a distance you've run many times, and with the realization that you can walk that far, there is the knowledge that success will come.

A crossroads is that juncture where a choice of direction is made. The road that crosses goes somewhere else, a diversion. It is the wrong way on this day, but there will be crossroads in disguise, where difficult choices must be made, intersections that offer new directions and you must be prepared to choose.

In the shorter runs, you decide when to use more speed, when to make a move, when to lead, when to follow. The short run requires wit, the long run determination, and you will be running them simultaneously, for in the great course of living there are many small portions which comprise the whole.

The crossroad puzzle is not difficult for the enlightened and you will learn its costume, breaking bewildering problems down to the lowest common denominators for better understanding, a toy taken apart to see how it works. It is in reassembling that you will learn solution to baffling circumstances, a thoughtful analysis that will serve you well, for a disguise is only an alteration and a trick. The true nature of everything is always present, if only to be discovered.

And such is the nature of this run, to discover, to learn, to remove your disguise, and you will better understand how best to choose your direction.

Mile 25

You are running the longest mile of the marathon, the mile before excitement.

A mile of patience, absolute control, the challenge to be steady, to persevere. There are still more than 1700 strides ... 5,280 feet left in this mile, with another to follow, but you are quietly assured, doubt gone.

The spirit of this portion is knowing joy will come in the next. There are so many tomorrows and joy in each. Tomorrow is anticipation, wonderment, love, for much happiness comes with the morrow and achievement starts with each beginning.

No buoyancy in the legs, hard spots where muscles once responded easily, but a little faster and you will finish quicker, but not too much faster, just gradual improvement. Body consuming, dying minutely, but the soul lives, new determination swells. Destiny ahead, each moment a brick, each step the mortar, brick by brick, step by step, completion nearing.

Ahead, people gathered and two other runners just making a gradual turn to the right, like a film in slow motion. You're gaining!

Flailing an arm at those who shout encouragement, you estimate the distance at perhaps 50 yards, half of a football field. If you've been gaining, they've been running slower, so it figures you will catch them with a continuous pace. And one has stopped! Bent over, stretching. He's had it. You know he will struggle to finish.

"Hang in there," you tell him as you pass.

"Thanks," was his simple reply. "I'll make it."

The other runner is also struggling, the gap cut in half, and it is difficult to maintain caution. The realization you've run a good race, that there's plenty left for the final distance, is wondrous, and you approach the slowly moving runner.

"You okay?"

"Yeah, but I'm cramping."

You feel like a winner, passing others, moving faster, not even minding the rise in the road, and there's still another runner, perhaps a quarter mile away.

You will try.

Mile 26

Z eal.

Pursuing the final runner, a last challenge, and with eyes trained on the spindly figure, you move doggedly.

A quickening, a mental loosening, clear acknowledgement the body is going to be okay. Mind smiling, a satisfaction, knowing what is ahead, just ahead.

The marathon deserves no mercy. It gives none. There will be none.

The brain wants to let the body go as you taste and prepare, readying, feet tapping. What pleasure in holding this engine in check, nearly out of coal but chugging in on time.

Feet consuming, brain urging, sinew responding, the measure narrowing between two single figures gasping for fulfillment. You have trained well, could have run harder, but there will be other days, other runs, you take this day with gladness.

The other runner is now barely moving. "Not far now," you encourage, "Hang in there." He's hurting, jogging with a pronounced limp, muscles cramping.

No response. He is beaten in this contest of two, a swordsman pierced, but the wound will not stop him. He will stagger but he will live.

You know how he feels, but you're strong, savor this, revel in it, feel the wonderment of it, as you stride toward destiny.

Flags fluttering, the final turn. People applauding, encouraging while awaiting another still on the course, but you are here, you are now, and with a surge you rush past and turn into the path.

"Now entering the stadium...", the loudspeaker blares ...

Pushing, forcing, testing to the limit after nearly 26 miles, a gaunt messenger gasps as he enters the final phase of his mission.

With arm aloft, a knight atop a charging steed, the victor strides with painful grace, a grimacing lope. Just a little more, a little more. A little while and you will have lived, and died, and conquered, and shall be reborn.

385 yards

Adrenalin flowing, excitement soaring.
So long have you been patient, now let it go!
Flailing, roaring, a crescendo of emotion
hurtling to conclusion.

Thrusting down the track,
around a turn, then another,
and a final sprint, then
thrusting across the finish line.

You are changed.
You are forever more a new being
with unspoken strength.

The spirits of all who preceded
welcome you.
You are a marathoner.

Photo credits

Cover photo by Bruce Morrison.
Mile 1 photo, l-r, Mary Lou Day, Phil Roberts, Terry Campbell.
Mile 2 photo of Don Coffman, by Sailer Ltd.
Mile 3 photo of Cheryl Boessow by Huntsville Track Club.
Mile 4 photo, l-r, David Samuel, Mark Walsh.
Mile 5 photo by Bruce Morrison.
Mile 6 photo of Robin Fondren.
Mile 7 photo of Diane Brewer.
Mile 8 photo of Wes Wessley by Sailer Ltd.
Mile 9 photo of Rosa Mota by Sailer Ltd.
Mile 10 photo of Gabrielle Anderson by Sailer Ltd.
Mile 11 photo of Joan Nesbit by Ley Gorrell.
Mile 12 photo of Norm Green by Sailer Ltd.
Mile 13 photo by Bruce Morrison.
Mile 14 photo of John Campbell by Sailer Ltd.
Mile 15 photo of Priscilla Welch by Sailer Ltd.
Mile 16 photo by Bruce Morrison.
Mile 17 photo by Bruce Morrison.
Mile 18 photo by Thomas G. Wilson III.
Mile 19 photo of Takashi Yagisawa by Bruce Morrison.
Mile 20 photo, l-r, Lindsey Bodden, Claudia Ciavarella.
Mile 21 photo of Neil Riemenschneider by Pam Bailey.
Mile 22 photo of Tony Bateman by Bruce Morrison.
Mile 23 photo at Blue-Grey 10K, Lake City, Florida.
Mile 24 photo, l-r, Randall Roland (117), Dewayne Satterfield.
Mile 25 photo of Nancy Grayson by Bruce Morrison.
Mile 26 photo of Bill Rodgers by Bruce Morrison.
385 photo of Bob Schlau by Sailer Ltd.

All photos are from the files of *Running Journal*

Bruce Morrison is a veteran writer, editor, publisher — and runner. He is chief operating officer of Media Services Group, headquartered in Greeneville, Tennessee, which manages newspapers, specialty publications, and radio stations.

He and his wife, Julie, founded Running Journal, a publication which covers running, racewalking, and triathlon events in the southern and southeastern United States. Running Journal sponsors the oldest running grand prix in America, a series of races held throughout the southeast each year from Parkersburg, West Virginia, to Fort Myers, Florida.

Prior to moving to Tennessee, he published daily newspapers in Selma, Alabama and Concord, North Carolina, and was managing editor for dailies in Cadillac, Michigan and Natchez, Mississippi. He was born in West Palm Beach, Florida but moved to Gladstone, Michigan in the Upper Peninsula at age 10, and to Milwaukee, Wisconsin at age 13.

"I was fascinated with language as a child and wanted to be a writer when I grew up. I've chased some rainbows and caught a few — and there are others on the horizon. I've learned there are different ways to attainment, though. The most practical, and normal, approach is one step at a time. Occasionally, if you're prepared, you can take a quantum step," Morrison said.

"I believe if you can run a marathon, you can accomplish anything. You can't just decide to run one, though, because it will whip the unprepared. When I finished my first one, I had to walk and run the last nine miles. Once during those final, grueling miles I yelled aloud that I would finish if I had to crawl. After I crossed the finish line, I cried with relief at the realization of what I'd done. I had conquered myself."

26.2: Trail of Truth is available to running clubs and organizations at quantity discount prices.

Contact:

Pete Tortolini, Marketing Director
Hampton Roads Publishing Co., Inc.
891 Norfolk Square
Norfolk, VA 23502

804-459-2453 [For information]

800-766-8009 [To order]